Lovely Dreams

Tammye Dearing

Copyright © 2024 by Tammye Dearing
ISBN: 978-1-77883-485-1 (Paperback)

All rights reserved. No part of this publication may be reproduced, distributed, or transmitted in any form or by any means, including photocopying, recording, or other electronic or mechanical methods, without the prior written permission of the publisher, except in the case brief quotations embodied in critical reviews and other noncommercial uses permitted by copyright law.

The views expressed in this book are solely those of the author and do not necessarily reflect the views of the publisher, and the publisher hereby disclaims any responsibility for them.

BookSide Press
877-741-8091
www.booksidepress.com
orders@booksidepress.com

Preface:

This is a dream that I had (couldn't get it out of my head, for over a week), and thought it was a great story. It was moving enough that I was in tears when I woke up June 9, 2011. It was while in Las Vegas on vacation. The dream was so real, that it had to be written down and shared. Even as I read it today, I fight back the tears of joy!

Dedication:

I dedicate this book to my Lord, for giving me the desire and passion to write, to my momma, Linda Lindsey, for always believing in me and my passions, to my husband, Marvin Dearing, for having faith in me and believing in my ability as a writer, and my lifelong friend, Roby Rowland, that pushed me to write the dream down and submit it for publishing.

STORY:

It started out that a peasant girl, somewhere in England, wanted to go for a swim in a very calm river. As she swam underwater toward her destination, a castle on the side of the river, the water was very clear, she felt a real threat in the water and came up to have a look around. There was a wall just up from her on the left with a dense forest between it and the castle. This forest only lasted a short distance. Past that were vast lush green meadows. Nothing looked very threatening, so she went back underwater to continue her journey. As she swam, she met a very handsome gentleman with red hair, about her age, that motioned her forward and took her hand. He swam with her until she reached the edge of the castle. She noticed as long as she held his hand there was no reason to come up for air. Just as they got to the edge of the castle, he let her hand go,

nodded, and swam away. She got out of the river, went into the castle, re-dressed, and went to work cleaning as a housemaid. At the end of the day, she would put that mornings clothing back on, and go back to the river, where the young man would be waiting. He never talked, just took her hand and escorted her through the ominous part of the water. After a time of this daily ritual, maybe a couple months, one morning on her way to work, just before she got out of the water, but while still swimming, he gave her a very sweet tender kiss on the lips. After this she really looked forward to their daily trips. He was never inappropriate, just light kisses, holding hands, and with great admiration for each other in their eyes. One day, about a month after the first kiss, the Lord of the castle bought the girl for taxes owed by her parents. She had been working there to try and pay these off, but they kept owing more and more until they sold her to the Lord. This paid their bill, so now she belonged to the Lord of the castle. The Lord requested that she not go swimming in the river for the fear that something would happen to her. This would be a great loss to him, for she was now his property for a large sum of money owed him by her parents. This perplexed the young peasant girl. She would go to the bank of the river every morning and night looking for her friend. She was not allowed to go past the edge of the castle or enter the water, and she knew he wasn't allowed to pass the edge of the forest or come on land, so she became very sad and withdrawn from everyone. This was because he

was the only one that had made her happy. She went through her daily chores, as told, and retired to her chamber without eating nighty for several months. One evening before retiring the Lord of the castle asked her help attending one of his parties. He introduced her to a whole lot of people, in which she would be working. She, as well as, the people she was introduced to were to serve food and beverages to people that he thought were friends and people in which he thought he found favor. There was a girl around her age, named Samantha, with long golden-brown wavy hair. They became fast friends. Samantha quickly showed her the ropes, and introduced her to another of her friends, a young gentleman, also around their age with light brown hair, and beautiful hazel eyes. He was quite the looker, but with all that he had going for him, he was mute. This in turn wasn't a problem, since she had friends when she was quite young, that were also mute. She'd had a lady teach her some sign language, and what she didn't know how to sign she could spell. The young fellow, as far as they knew, didn't have a name, everyone called him "Boy". Samantha called him Ky It was easy to say and spell. This had been one of her Uncle's names, and she thought quite fondly of him, as she did their friend. Samantha and the peasant girl became close friends after the party, and spent loads of time together, always with Ky by their side. The three of them would spend their off evenings along the river bank, in the meadows laughing and playing, collecting flowers, and just enjoying their friendship. The peasant

girl was very glad for their chance meeting. Ky and she talked as much as they could, given her limitations of sign language, and became very fond of him. After a time, he became quite upset that he could not express himself to her, as he wanted, because of her limitations. This upset the girl tremendously, hurting her feelings. She had to do something to fix the problem. She hated seeing him so frustrated and upset. It hurt even more since, she had feelings for him, but would not allow him or anyone ever to know, or allow herself to acknowledge these feelings for anyone ever again, since she had lost her best friend in the water. Whom she still missed so very deeply. That afternoon she told Samantha of her dilemma, they asked the Lord if they might have a couple of hours to go into the market for supplies. The Lord gave them a list of needs, and the full afternoon to shop the market. They walked to town, as young girls do, in high spirits, gathering what was needed on the list. Once done, they found an old bookstore of second hand and deleted books. The keeper of the store, after a time, asked if she could help them find something. They told her of their problem, and she went on an expedition of the back of the store. In little while, she came running out of the back saying she had found what they needed with great enthusiasm. It was an old school book from the university of sign language. She said it had been her daughter's, and there was no charge. They were so elated that she had found it that they both hugged her neck, and raced from the little shop, down the road, and back to the castle.

Samantha also needed to learn more signing, so for several weeks they would sneak into one another's chambers to study, staying up late, after their time with Ky. Their friend soon began to see their progress in sign and became very pleased with them. He was so happy to be able to communicate better, that he began to open up to them a little more. The peasant girl began noticing very small, subtle similarities to her friend in the water. It was all in her head, or so she thought it was just a coincidence. He was kind, easy to be around, full of life, but she would not allow herself to feel for him, just because he reminded her of her friend in the water, not even after so much time had passed. She still longed for his touch and to see him again. One night Samantha had left, she heard a quiet knock at the door. She asked who it was. No reply. Suddenly, there were three more knocks. She asked again, still no reply. She realized it had to be Ky, so she opened the door, looked both ways down the hall, and pulled him into her chamber. He told her he would be leaving soon, and wanted to ask if she would escort him when he left. He had three days before he was to leave, and each day he would tell her a little more. She, of course, accepted and wondered if he had told Samantha. He signed, no he had not told her, and asked her not to tell her either, that he would tell her why later. He then slipped out the door and down the hall. So, each day they spent as normal, and each night after Samantha and she studied, he would come to her chamber, knock three times, and let himself in after he checked the corridor,

The first night, he told of how his friendship had started with Samantha. How she had found him in the streets, befriended him, and brought him to the castle to see if the Lord may allow him to work for room and board. The Lord was very kind-hearted, he needed a few more servants, and agreed. This was three or four weeks after the peasant girl was bought from her parents. He told of how she had helped him to learn how to dress properly, wash himself daily to be presentable, how to address the Lord respectfully, do daily chores, and proper procedures. He was very thankful for her friendship, but feared if he told her he was leaving she would be upset.

The second night, he told the peasant girl of his childhood, how his parents were so stern, how they were always in their work with no time for him, how he spent a lot of time solely on his own, how he had met a very special friend he was very close to, and one day that person was just gone. He searched for weeks and never found them. He felt very lost, abandoned, and alone until he left his home and met Samantha. She had brought him here, but was not sure how his parents had found him, now he had to return to tend the family business. He had gotten permission from the Lord for her to escort him. She was very sad. He then told her he would come for her the next morning for his departure, said his goodbyes, and started for the door. The girl caught his shoulder and told him she did not want him to go. She wanted him to stay, since they only had one more night and part of a day left. He

stayed and held her very close all night. She never felt as safe, yet so horribly upset in her life. Her heart felt as if it were going to burst, or someone was ripping it out of her chest. Sometime during the night, she slipped off to a restless sleep.

The next morning, he shook her gently, and asked if he could blindfold her until they reached his parents. She reluctantly agreed. He took her hand, the touch gave her goosebumps. Something was familiar in that touch. She could not quite put her finger on exactly what it was. Soon they halted. He was standing in the river when he removed the blindfold. His hair was turning from light brown to a gorgeous red, his face was transforming into a face she never thought she would see again. He was her friend from the water, that she loved, and missed so miserably for so long! She had found so many of the same attributes in the young man, that she knew in the friend from the water, but would dismiss them as coincidence. She was so in love with her friend from the water that she would not allow herself to feel that way for another. She had fallen so deeply in love that she overlooked all of the signs in front of her. She now was so shocked and elated that she was absolutely speechless. She threw her arms around his neck and jumped into his arms, kissing him all over. After she calmed down, he began walking further out into the water with her in tow. Then she heard the most beautiful sound she had ever heard in her life. He started actually talking! She was so surprised! He began telling her of how his heart had broken, how he

longed to see her again, how he had gotten permission to go on land to see if he could locate her and find if what he thought they had was real. He told her about not being able to speak in a language others could understand, so he used sign language, and by her doing everything she could to learn to communicate with him that he could tell how fond she was of him. He also could tell she was holding back and had seen her going to the river every morning and night still looking for him even though it had been such a long time. He knew then that what they had was real. He told her that he had paid her debt to the Lord, and his parents hadn't found him, they had passed on to the other life, that he wanted a life with her if she would have him. She of course accepted. He summoned a waterwitch to help turn her into a being from the water so as they may live together in the river, sea, or ocean.

Epilogue:

This is when I woke up for real, tightly snuggled into my bed, crying and trying to fight the tears. All over a dream!

www.ingramcontent.com/pod-product-compliance
Lightning Source LLC
LaVergne TN
LVHW051936070526
838200LV00078B/4976